This book is dedicated to the courageous children everywhere who will one day change the world—especially my son Koa.

The child in me forever thanks my parents, who recognized and encouraged my gift of writing from a young age:

- Thanks to my mother, Frances Collier, for raising me to believe that I can do anything.

- Thanks to my father, Charles Reynolds, for teaching me to "dig deep" and that anything worth doing is worth doing well.

www.mascotbooks.com

**Sylvester Lou Goes Beyond the Mountain:
A Linx Land Adventure**

©2023 Keisha Reynolds. All Rights Reserved. No part of this publication may be reproduced, stored in a retrieval system or transmitted in any form by any means electronic, mechanical, or photocopying, recording or otherwise without the permission of the author.

For more information, please contact:
Mascot Kids, an imprint of Amplify Publishing Group
620 Herndon Parkway, Suite 320
Herndon, VA 20170
info@mascotbooks.com

Library of Congress Control Number: 2021912813

CPSIA Code: PRKF0423A

ISBN-13: 978-1-64543-505-1

Printed in China

Sylvester Lou
Goes Beyond the Mountain
A Linx Land Adventure

*To: Elliot Jane
Don't be afraid to be different!
Keisha*

WRITTEN BY:
Keisha Reynolds

ILLUSTRATED BY: E. JOO
LAYOUT BY: ASHLEY STOPERA

It is not very easy being a Linx.
Four legs like a dog, with skin like a sphinx.

Large eyes like an owl and an orange toucan beak,
That sometimes interferes when the Linx goes to speak.

Flopped ears like a mouse, and as a matter of fact,
You couldn't handle looking like that!

But for all of the Linx, looks didn't matter at all,
They looked somewhat the same, stood the same feet tall.

To tell them apart was a huge task you see,
They decided long ago that the same they would be.

So every third day of every third week,
The Mayor would come;
the Linx creed he would speak:

"Same are the Linx, and same we will do.
There is no difference between you and you.

"We live in the same houses, we have the same cars,
We gaze at the same time each night to the stars.

"Everything is alike, and alike is most fair,
We have no worries or ridiculous cares.

"Our one and only Linx Golden Rule:
Beware and be careful in all that you do,

"To avoid at all costs the likeness of man,
Be sure every Linx to do all that you can.

"To heed every word—we do so beseech,
To keep out his sight and far out his reach.

"This is our pledge—an oath to behold,
Let safety be our story—not stories untold.

"I promise, I swear, and hold my hand high,
I do it each third week and vow not to die."

So back to their houses, every Linx would go,
With like Linx ideas and like Linx no-no's.

If there's one little thing that every Linx knew:
Steer clear of man and all he could do.

But there's one little problem they hadn't figured out;

Divided by a river as best they could see,

All hidden by a mountain, it let them stay free.

But water they needed to live their lives too,

They would sneak to the river, and here's what they'd do.

Every child got a pot, every grown-up, a pail.
They filled them twice high, every child, female, male.

What else could a Linx do to maintain?
Water was essential—its need was made plain.

For washing and cleaning and cooking and drinking,
Each Linx knew their task and did without thinking.

So on river days of every month, this is what they would do,
Till one day, along came lil' Sylvester Lou.

He hated doing things exactly the same,
But his parents did drill *same* right into his brain.

It caused him to hide and sometimes to sneak,
To avoid doing the same things each day of the week.

He went to the river on a non-river day and said,
All the wonderful wonderings he held in his head.

He felt in a sense that his life was all through,
'Cause after all, he's a Linx, and he'd do as they'd do.

But just as he started to come out of his daze,
A mountain he noticed had captured his gaze.

All sorts of things started into his mind,
He wondered at once what lay just behind.

"I wonder if I should take just a wee bitty peek?
A Linx is not a coward; a Linx is not meek."

So over the mountain he decided to go,
Forgetting the creed and his Linx no-no's.

On the other side of the mountain, guess what he saw?
A strangely wonderful different kind of law.

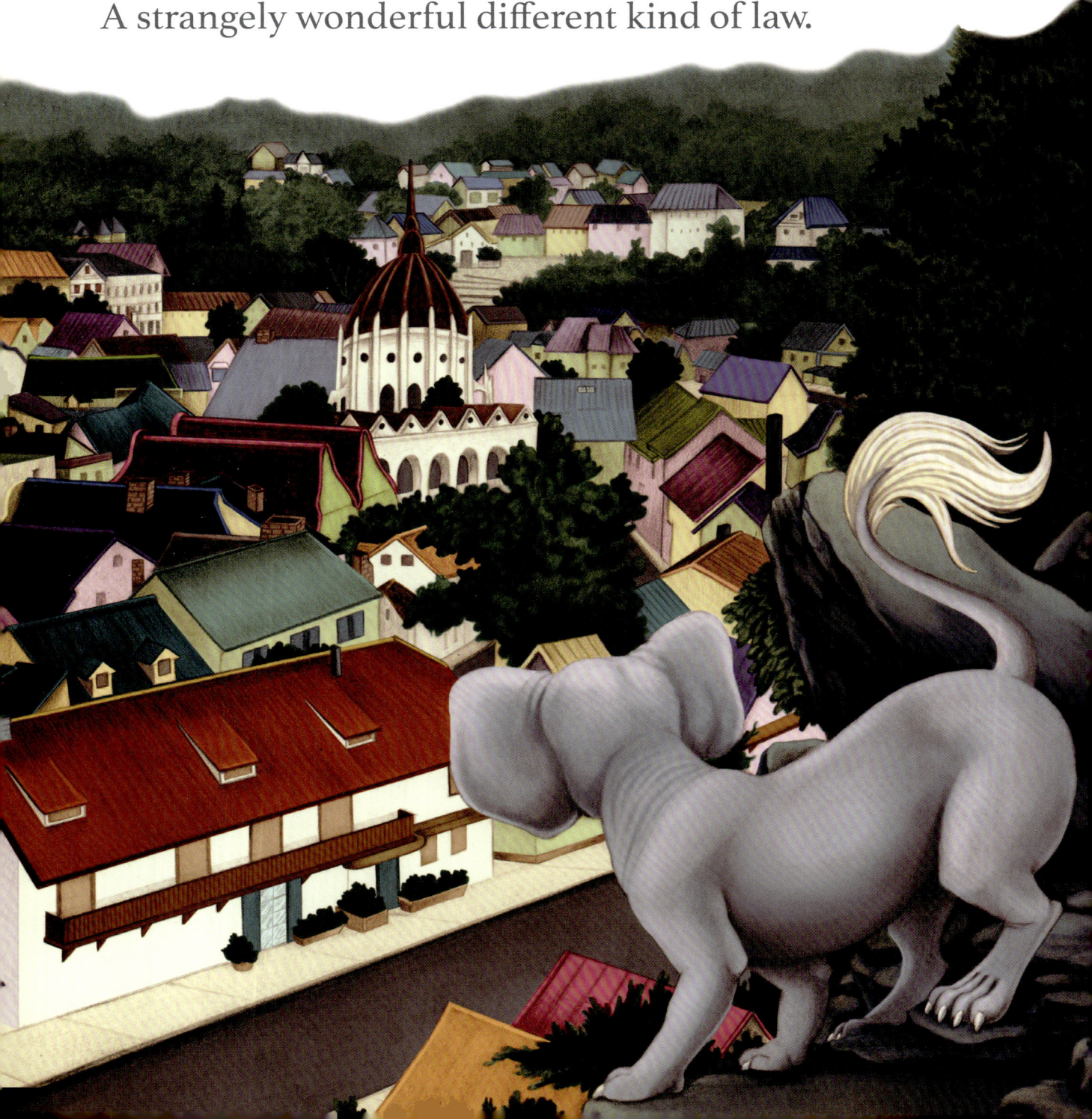

Everything was varied: pink, purple, and blue,
Everything looked so different, everything so new.

For twenty minutes more, Sylvester couldn't speak,
With his mouth open wide, he stood in the street.

He forgot to be frightened; no, he wasn't at all,
When a human boy spoke, "Hey, pass me my ball."

Sylvester Lou Linx gave the ball a slight kick,
And the next thing he knew, he was playing with Nick.

They talked of their differences and the Land of the Linx,
Sylvester Lou's description gave Nick a slight wince.

"I could not imagine having the same that, the same this,
I am five-foot-two and my brother, six-six.

"No, I can't imagine ever being the same,
So much you miss out on—too much to name.

"People come in all colors, sizes, and shapes.
Every person an art of this world's landscape."

Then Nick looked real serious, more man than boy,
"How will you know when difference is joy?"

Then his mouth continued speaking
before Sylvester could reply,

"I will tell you how, and I will not lie."

"When every day changes in small little ways,
You can have ice cream tomorrow and popcorn today.

"When every new person brings new views you'll see,
A new day, a new hope of what life will be.

"But my friend, don't let me make up your mind,
You are welcome to come and see life with my kind."

And with that Sylvester Lou followed the boy,
With his different ideas and his different human toy.

Meanwhile in Linx Land, the same wasn't the same.
They were missing a Linx—Sylvester Lou was his name.

So in every Linx corner, they searched in defeat,
With thoughts entering minds—was he eaten by the beast?

They knew they had warned lil' Sylvester Lou,
Just exactly what it was that those man-beasts could do.

They walk on two legs and stand tall like a tree,
Oh, there's no telling where their little Linx could be.

All hearts were heavy, especially the Lou mom and dad,
Oh, nothing good will come of this; this story's too sad.

Perhaps the best outcome of what they thought they knew,
Was that man trapped Sylvester and put him in a zoo.

So all through the night they prepared to attack,

To climb that old mountain and get Sylvester Lou back.

And when morning came, they gathered in town,
They listened as the Mayor droned on with a frown.

Then after warnings he begged them to heed,
He led all the Linx into the Linx creed.

Then they swam across that river with beaks held high,
And climbed that ole mountain with their eyes to the sky.

When they reached the other side, no words they could speak,
The Mayor's little heart skipped a beat, he did think.

But nevertheless, to the creed he stayed true,
He roused every Linx with what they should do.

They marched into town, in a line, three by three,
They would fight till the end—until Sylvester was free.

But on a great field they came to a halt,
There stood Sylvester—was he under assault?

Sylvester looked back toward the Linx and said,
"What are they going to do? I have so much dread,"
Was just one of the ponderings within his Linx head.

He stood with Nick's family and was not dismayed,
"We really should hear what the Linx came to say."

But deep in his heart he knew what the Linx thought true,
They believed he was stolen, who knows what they'd do?

But all of a sudden, someone took to the floor,

It was a human Mayor who stood four-foot-four.

"Dear Linx, I thought this day we never would see,
A time when you and us could at the same place be.

"We did not, never ever, steal a Linx child away.
He came on his own but has brought us this day.

"We wish to be friends and help one another,
We want to be different but still call you our brother."

And all the while, as this little man spoke,
The Linx were confused, could this be a joke?

The Linx Mayor chose just this time to chime in,
"My friends, he's a liar, a master of spin."

"But they did not attack," one Linx did dare speak.
"And what about his wanting for mutual peace?"

"I don't see any evil in all that they do,"
Shouted out from the crowd lil' Sylvester Lou.

"There is no wrong in being so different,
Here's my friend Nick, and he is insistent,

"That we can be friends no matter our looks,
We can share secrets, playtime, and even our books.

"I wasn't stolen to this faraway land,
I came on my own and saw all that I can.

"I always wanted to be a singer," said Sylvester Lou,
"But I was a Linx and planned to do what you do.

"But no longer do I wish to endure,
A life that is the same—no magic, no gore.

"So I will stay here, if that is the plan,
To have the same stay the same, in all of Linx Land."

But one after one, then two after two,
Every Linx spoke up on what he wanted to do.

Well shocked was the Mayor of little Linx Land,
He finally discovered every Linx had a plan,

Of something else they thought they would be,
Definitely not the same—surely that he could see.

So he made the decision to change the Linx creed,
"If difference is what you want, different we will be.

"I can't remember why the same we wanted to stay,
Except to say, that my grandfather's grandfather taught it that way.

"On this here day, we will officially be,

Friends with all of man and different to see."

So every fourth day of every fourth week,
The Linx and the humans would gather in streets.

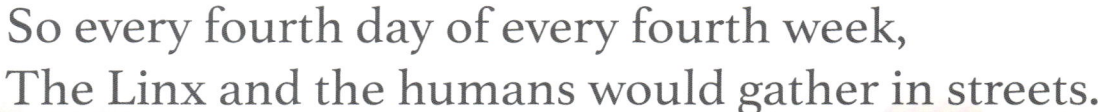

They would sing; they would dance, laugh, play, and preach,
But most of all to one another they would teach.

Not by lessons, textbooks, or plans,
But through shared joy and helping hands.

Oh, little Linx Land, the same it will never be,

Sylvester Lou sparked a change with his yearning to be free.

So nowadays you'll find him, mostly here or sometimes there,
Singing for the crowds, without a worry or care.

He can be heard near or far—in whichever land,

With a song in his heart and a mic in his hand.

About the Author

Keisha Reynolds

Keisha believes in the power of a dream—those that we reach for in our hearts, and those we witness during our sleep. It has always been a dream for Keisha to share her writings with the world. It's no wonder Sylvester Lou's character first appeared to Keisha in her dream one night, and this book is the result.

Keisha first discovered her love of words through poetry at age seven when it poured out of her one day, before she even knew what she had written. That day ignited a passion in her for writing that will never go away. She started imagining and typing short stories to share with her friends and family. Words continue to live deep in her heart and it is why she has built a communications career and business that heavily includes writing.

In 2022, Keisha relocated within the United States from Maryland to the island of Puerto Rico with her husband, Lenny, and their son, Koa. Recently, Keisha authored an essay in *Chicken Soup for the Soul: Listen to Your Dreams*, published in 2020. During her free time, she enjoys podcasting and currently hosts a show called *Global Warriors*, featuring world changers and more. She also enjoys reading, writing, creating art, and is a spiritual healer, teacher, and practitioner in Reiki, Theta, and Yoga.

Check out printable pages and Sylvester Lou items at:
www.SylvesterLou.com

For additional information about the author, visit:
www.KeishaReynolds.com